A Note to Parents

W9-BJP-620

Reading books aloud and playing word games are two valuable ways parents can help their children learn to read. The easy-to-read stories in the **My First Hello Reader! With Flash Cards** series are designed to be enjoyed together. Six activity pages and 16 flash cards in each book help reinforce phonics, sight vocabulary, reading comprehension, and facility with language. Here are some ideas to develop your youngster's reading skills:

Reading with Your Child

- Read the story aloud to your child and look at the colorful illustrations together. Talk about the characters, setting, action, and descriptions. Help your child link the story to events in his or her own life.
- Read parts of the story and invite your child to fill in the missing parts. At first, pause to let your child "read" important last words in a line. Gradually, let your child supply more and more words or phrases. Then take turns reading every other line until your child can read the book independently.

Enjoying the Activity Pages

- Treat each activity as a game to be played for fun. Allow plenty of time to play.
- Read the introductory information aloud and make sure your child understands the directions.

Using the Flash Cards

- Read the words aloud with your child. Talk about the letters and sounds and meanings.
- Match the words on the flash cards with the words in the story.
- Help your child find words that begin with the same letter and sound, words that rhyme, and words with the same ending sound.
- Challenge your child to put flash cards together to make sentences from the story and create new sentences.

Above all else, make reading time together a fun time. Show your child that reading is a pleasant and meaningful activity. Be generous with your praise and know that, as your child's first and most important teacher, you are contributing immensely to his or her command of the printed word.

—Tina Thoburn, Ed. D.
Educational Consultant

Copyright © 1994 by Nancy Hall, Inc.
All rights reserved. Published by Scholastic Inc.
MY FIRST HELLO READER!, CARTWHEEL BOOKS, and the
CARTWHEEL BOOKS logo are registered trademarks of Scholastic Inc.
The MY FIRST HELLO READER! logo is a registered trademark of Scholastic Inc.

Library of Congress Cataloging-in-Publication Data
Packard, Mary.
    Bubble trouble / by Mary Packard; illustrated by Elena Kucharik.
        p.   cm.—(My first hello reader!)
    "Cartwheel books."
    "With flash cards."
    Summary: A boy makes bubbles all day long until he makes a mess and it's time
to clean up.
    ISBN 0-590-48513-X
    [1. Bubbles—Fiction. 2. Stories in rhyme.]
    I. Kucharik, Elena, ill. II. Title. III. Series.
PZ8.3.P125Bu   1994
[E]—dc20   94-16975
                                                                         CIP
                                                                          AC
12 11 10   6 7 8 9/9

Printed in the U.S.A.   24

First Scholastic printing, November 1994

BUBBLE
TROUBLE

by Mary Packard

Illustrated by Elena Kucharik

My First Hello Reader!
With Flash Cards

SCHOLASTIC INC.

New York   Toronto   London   Auckland   Sydney

I make bubbles in the air.

I make bubbles in my hair.

I make bubbles big and round…

and listen for the popping
sound.

See the bubbles in the sink.

Hear the bubbles in my drink.

I make bubbles here

and there.

I make bubbles everywhere!

Here's a bubble.

There's a bubble.

Sorry, Mom.

Am I in trouble?

Rhyme Time

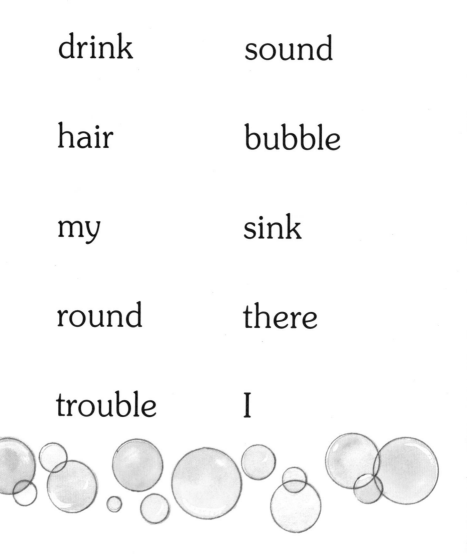

Rhyming words sound alike. Point to the words that rhyme with each other.

drink	sound
hair	bubble
my	sink
round	there
trouble	I

What Happens Next?

At the end of this story, the boy's mother sees all of the bubbles he has made.

How do you think his mother feels about the bubbles? Why do you think that?

What do you think happens next in the story?

Inside Story

Some words have smaller words in them. In each row, you can use your fingers to cover a letter or letters in the first word and make it look like the second word.

hair   air

sink   in

there   here

make   a

Big Bubbles

These children are blowing bubbles. The boy made a big bubble.

Point to two bubbles that are bigger.

Now point to the bubble that is the biggest.

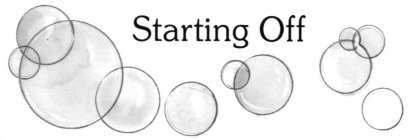

Starting Off

In each row, point to the word that begins with
the same letter as the first word in the row.

sink   see   in   round

make   here   my   for

big   sound bubble air

hair   for   and   here

there   trouble sink drink

Spring Cleaning

Emily is going to fill a bucket with soap bubbles to wash her bike.

Point to the things she would use.

Then point to the things she would not use.

Answers

(Rhyme Time)

drink   sound
hair   bubble
my   sink
round   there
trouble   I

(What Happens Next?) Answers will vary.

(Inside Story)

h **air**   **air**
s **in** k   **in**
t **here**   **here**
m **a** k e   **a**

(Big Bubbles)

bigger:    biggest:

(Starting Off)

sink   **see** in round
make   here **my** for
big   sound **bubble** air
hair   for and **here**
there   **trouble** sink drink

(Spring Cleaning)

She would use: She would not use: